Money Moves:
The Playbook for Building, Growing, and Protecting Your Wealth

Strategies for Smart Investing, Financial Freedom, and Lasting Legacy

By

Milton E. Brown, Jr., MBA

ISBN:
978-1-968973-52-0

Dedication

This book is dedicated to the everyday person who's done their best with what they've been given. To those who were never taught about money but took the leap to learn anyway. To those who've made mistakes, carried the weight of regret, and still chose to keep going. To the ones who've worked hard, lived paycheck to paycheck, raised families, and put others first, often at the cost of their own financial peace.

You may not have had all the tools, but you've always had the heart, and that matters. This is for the people who've read the articles, watched the videos, asked the questions, and yet still felt lost in a sea of opinions and conflicting advice. You kept searching anyway and never gave up.

Thank you for trusting me to walk beside you on this part of the journey. I hope this book speaks to you plainly, without judgment or hype. I hope it helps you see that financial freedom isn't just for others, it's for you, too.

Remember, every choice we make with our money produces a result. The good thing is you have the ability to influence those decisions, no matter how big or small. So, as you go through your financial journey, making many choices, just remember "Everything Costs…Can You Pay?"

Acknowledgement

Writing this book has been a journey shaped by countless conversations, experiences, and lessons learned over the years in the world of finance. I am deeply grateful to everyone who played a role in bringing this work to life.

To my clients, thank you for trusting me with your financial goals and allowing me to walk alongside you in your pursuit of financial clarity and independence. Your stories, challenges, and triumphs have inspired much of the insight shared in these pages.

To my mentors and colleagues in the financial advisory field, your guidance and collaboration have been invaluable. I've learned from your wisdom, your integrity, and your commitment to excellence. You've helped me grow not only as an advisor but as a lifelong student of financial stewardship.

To my editorial team and publishing partners, thank you for your patience, precision, and belief in this project. Your expertise helped shape this book into something I'm proud to share.

To my family and friends, your unwavering support has been my foundation. Thank you for encouraging me to pursue this endeavor, for understanding the late nights and early mornings, and for reminding me why this work matters.

And finally, to the reader, whether you're just beginning your financial journey or refining your strategy, I hope this book serves as a trusted companion. May it empower you to make informed decisions, build lasting wealth, and live with financial confidence.

With sincere gratitude,

Milton E. Brown, Jr., MBA

About the Author

With over two decades of experience in the financial industry, Milton E. Brown, Jr began his career with a simple but powerful mission: to understand how money works and how to create true financial freedom. That curiosity evolved into a lifelong passion for helping others take control of their financial futures.

Over the years, he has successfully built multiple seven-figure businesses, demonstrating that the principles he teaches are not just theory, they work in the real world. Today, he is the founder and principal advisor of his own financial advisory firm, where he specializes in retirement planning through his proprietary platform, The Serenity Retirement System. This proven approach has helped countless clients navigate the complexities of retirement with confidence and peace of mind.

Dedicated to empowering individuals and families, he conducts free Financial Literacy Workshops focused on financial planning fundamentals and asset protection, ensuring that sound financial education is accessible to all. His commitment to service extends beyond his professional life; along with his wife, he established the Jaden Sebastian Blake Foundation in loving memory of their son, whom they lost in an automobile accident, to carry on his legacy of promoting blood and organ donation. The JSB Foundation also provides scholarships to college students.

Married and the proud father of five children, he understands firsthand the importance of building a secure future for the people you love. His work is driven by a deep belief that financial freedom is not just about wealth, it's about living a life of purpose, security, and generosity.

Table of Contents

Chapter 1
Credit – More Than Just a Number

Unlock the Power of Your Score and Stop Letting It Judge You

Your credit score isn't just for loans; it's your financial reputation. This chapter breaks down how to build it, boost it, and use it like a VIP pass to better deals and smarter decisions.

Let's be honest, credit can feel like one of those mysterious, intimidating, adult things nobody really explains. But it doesn't have to be. Your credit score isn't just a boring number on a report, it's kind of like your financial rep sheet. This chapter is here to help you understand what's "actually" going on behind those digits, and how you can use credit as a tool instead of letting it stress you out.

So, what is Credit?

At its core, credit is all about trust. It's the ability to borrow money or get things now (like a car, apartment, or phone) with the promise that you'll pay it back later. When you use credit responsibly, you're basically telling lenders, "Hey, you can trust me." Over time, all your borrowing and repayment habits get collected into something called your credit history, which is then turned into a score to provide a quick snapshot of how reliable you've been with money.

But here's the thing: your credit isn't just about loans or credit cards. It can impact everything from the interest rates you get to whether you land that apartment or even that job.

How Credit Reporting Works
(Without the Boring Jargon)

Credit reporting is the backbone of your financial identity. It begins with the interactions you have with lenders, banks, credit card companies, and service providers. Every time you engage in a financial agreement, whether you're approved for a new line of credit, make a timely payment, or fall behind, those actions are documented and reported to credit bureaus.

However, this process is far more structured and standardized than most people realize. Let's walk through each step in more detail:

1. *You Borrow or Use Credit*

This could mean anything from swiping a new credit card to financing a car or using a buy-now-pay-later app. When you do that, you're basically saying, "Yep, I'm okay with this being reported to credit bureaus." Even just applying for something can count; those are called hard inquiries, and yep, they can slightly impact your score for a bit.

2. *Your Behavior Gets Tracked*

Once your account is open, your financial habits start getting recorded. Think:

- Are you paying on time?
- How much credit are you using?
- Do you have any collections or judgments?
- Are you opening lots of new accounts?

Each action you take is like a data point being recorded in your financial diary.

3. *Lenders Report Your Activity*

Most lenders update the credit bureaus every month, sometimes more often. They share info like:

- Your balance
- If you paid on time (or didn't)
- The status of the account (in good standing, late, in collections)
- Any significant changes, such as credit line increases or settlements

Heads up, not all lenders report to all three credit bureaus. So, don't be surprised if things look a little different on each one.

4. *The Bureaus Update Your Credit Report*

These agencies collect everything into your personal file, which includes:

- Your name, address, and Social Security number
- Your open and closed accounts
- Public records (like bankruptcies or liens)
- Any collection activity
- Inquiries from lenders

Mistakes happen! That's why it's a smart move to check your report regularly and make sure it's all accurate.

5. *Your Score Gets Recalculated*

Once your info is updated, it gets fed into scoring models (like FICO or Vantage Score), which spit out your current score. It can change month-to-month depending on what's new.

Things like:

- Paying down a credit card
- Opening a new account
- Missing a payment
- Getting something negative removed

Your Credit Isn't Set in Stone

This whole cycle refreshes every 30 days, depending on when your lenders report. So, your credit score is always shifting —it reflects what's happening *right now* with your money habits.

Why All This Matters

Before giving you a loan or an apartment, people want to know if they can trust you financially. That's where your credit report comes in. It's a track record of how dependable you are on paying your debts.

So, What Exactly Is a Credit Bureau?

Think of a credit bureau as a kind of financial record-keeper.

Their whole job is to gather and organize information about how you handle credit, like your loans, credit cards, payment history, and even how often you apply for new accounts.

They collect this info from places like banks, lenders, credit card companies, and other financial institutions. Once they have all that data, they create something called a credit report, which is basically your financial report card.

Now here's where it matters:

Lenders (like banks or mortgage companies), landlords, and sometimes even employers check your credit report to get a feel for how trustworthy and financially responsible you are. Are you the type to pay bills on time? Do you max out your cards? Do you have a lot of debt?

It's fair to say that a credit bureau keeps track of how you manage your debt, and then (with your permission) shares that info with others so they can decide if they want to do business with you.

They're not judging you, they're just the messengers. And if you build good credit habits, they'll help you tell a great story.

Where Your Credit Report Comes From

Whenever someone talks about your "credit report," they're usually referring to one that comes from one of the big three credit bureaus: Experian, Equifax, or TransUnion.

Each of these companies does the same basic thing: they gather, organize, and report info about your financial life. But here's the twist: they don't all get the exact same information. Why? Because lenders and banks aren't required to report to all three bureaus.

So, one lender might send updates to Experian but not Equifax or TransUnion, which means your credit reports can look a little different depending on which bureau you're viewing.

Bottom line: it's totally normal if your reports (or even your scores) aren't identical across the board. That's just how the system works.

1. Experian "The Security-Savvy One"

Experian's kind of like the overachiever of the credit world. They cover all the basics: credit cards, loans, and payment history, but what really sets them apart is their focus on identity protection and credit monitoring.

If you've ever worried about someone stealing your info or opening an account in your name, Experian's got your back. They're big on tools that help you keep an eye on your credit and get notified fast if anything fishy happens. It's like having a security system for your financial life.

2. Equifax "The Data-Driven One"

Equifax has been in the credit game for a long time, and they've got some seriously deep roots when it comes to collecting and analyzing financial data. But here's something cool, not only do they track your credit history, but they also offer tools for employers. That means your job history might show up in your credit report, too. It helps lenders (and sometimes hiring managers) get a more complete picture of your background, financial, and professional. So yeah,

Equifax is kind of like the resume builder of the credit world.

3. *TransUnion "The Tech-Savvy One"*

TransUnion is all about credit, but with a modern twist. They still track the usual stuff like loans and credit cards, but they also lean into emerging tech and alternative data to give a more complete view of your financial life.

What does that mean for you? Well, your rental history or even utility payments might show up in your report, especially if you don't have a long credit history. It's a great way to show you're financially responsible, even if you're not a heavy credit card user.

TransUnion's goal is to make credit more inclusive and smarter, using tech to help people build trust with lenders in new ways.

Beyond the Big Three
Specialized Credit Reporting Agencies

So, aside from the major players, Experian, Equifax, and TransUnion, there are some specialized agencies that dig into more specific parts of your financial life. These guys don't track all your credit cards or loans like the big three do. Instead, they focus on specific financial activities, such as your banking habits, rental payments, utility bills, or even insurance claims.

These specialized bureaus really come into play when you're looking for services outside of traditional credit. For example, when you're trying to rent an apartment, your potential landlord might not just look at the standard credit report. They might check a rental reporting agency to see if you've consistently paid your rent on time or if you have any past evictions.

Similarly, if you apply for a checking account at a bank, they might pull a report from a company like ChexSystems. This report will show things like whether you've ever bounced a check or closed an account with negative balances.

In short, these specialized bureaus help create a deeper picture of who you are financially, beyond just your credit cards and loans. While you might not hear about these credit bureaus as much, they can have a big impact on your ability to rent a place, open a bank account, or even score affordable insurance rates.

By keeping an eye on these secondary reports and managing all your financial activities responsibly, you can build a stronger overall financial reputation, not just a higher credit score.

Here are six notable secondary bureaus:

1. Innovis "The Quiet Twin of the Big Three"

Innovis is kind of like the under-the-radar sibling of Experian, Equifax, and TransUnion. It tracks similar credit info, — things like your accounts, balances, and payment history, — but it doesn't get pulled as often when you're applying for loans or credit.

Instead, Innovis is mostly used behind the scenes for things like pre-approved credit cards or loan offers. So even if you've never checked your Innovis report, it's still out there, quietly doing its thing.

2. ChexSystems "The Bank Account Watchdog"

ChexSystems doesn't really care about your credit cards or loans it's all about your banking behavior. This bureau keeps track of things like overdrafts, bounced checks, unpaid fees, and even accounts you've closed with a negative balance.

So, if you've ever had trouble opening a new checking account and weren't sure why? ChexSystems might've been the reason. Banks use it to decide if you're a safe bet when it comes to handling a bank account responsibly.

It's kind of like a background check for your everyday money habits at the bank.

3. CoreLogic *"The Real Estate Reporter"*

CoreLogic is all about property-related stuff. If you've ever applied for a mortgage, rented a home, or been involved in anything housing-related, there's a good chance CoreLogic has some data on you.

They track things like your rental payment history, any evictions, and details tied to mortgage applications or ownership records. Landlords and mortgage lenders often check CoreLogic to get a better feel for how reliable you are when it comes to housing responsibilities

4. SageStream *"The Outside-the-Box Thinker"*

SageStream looks at your financial life a little differently. Instead of focusing only on traditional stuff like credit cards and loans, it gathers alternative credit data, meaning it checks out your non-traditional financial behavior.

That could include things like your cell phone payments, buy-now-pay-later activity, or other services where you're making regular payments but not necessarily using a credit card or loan.

SageStream is especially helpful for folks who don't have a long credit history. It helps lenders see that you're still responsible with money, even if you're not deep into the traditional credit system.

5. TeleCheck "The Check-Writer's Report Card"

Tele Check is all about your check-writing history—yep, actual paper checks. While checks aren't as common as they used to be, some retailers and banks still care about how you've handled them in the past.

TeleCheck tracks things like bounced checks, unpaid returned checks, or any fraud alerts tied to your checking activity. So, if you're trying to write a check at a store and it gets declined, chances are, TeleCheck had something to say about it behind the scenes.

If you still use checks regularly,or ever did—this is one report worth being aware of.

6. Lexis Nexis "

LexisNexis is a consumer reporting agency that provides financial and risk management data, but it operates differently from the major credit bureaus. Instead of focusing solely on credit history, LexisNexis gathers public records, legal filings, insurance claims, and other financial data to help businesses assess risk.

Some key aspects of LexisNexis:

- Public Records & Legal Data: Includes bankruptcy filings, liens, judgments, and property ownership records.

- Insurance & Fraud Prevention: Used by insurers to evaluate claims history and detect fraud.

- Identity Verification: Helps businesses confirm consumer identities for financial transactions.

Clarity Services "The Credit Helper for Underdogs"

Clarity Services is designed for folks who don't have much of a traditional credit history or maybe have hit a few bumps along the way. They specialize in subprime lending, which basically means helping lenders evaluate people with low or limited credit scores.

If you've ever applied for things like payday loans, installment loans, or short-term financing, Clarity might have been involved behind the scenes. They give lenders extra insight into your financial behavior beyond just what the big three bureaus show.

Think of Clarity as the bureau that says, "Hey, don't count this person out, they might still be creditworthy."

Why This Actually Matters

You could have a perfect credit report with Experian: on-time payments, low balances, the whole deal,—but still get denied for a bank account because of something sitting in ChexSystems.

It might be an old overdraft, a bounced check, or a closed account with a negative balance that's holding you back. That's why it's super important to keep an eye on all parts of your financial profile, not just your credit score.

The Six Key Ingredients That Makes Up Your Credit Score

So, How Is Your Credit Score Actually Calculated?

Your credit score isn't just some random number pulled out of thin air. It's built from your financial behavior, with each part of your money habits carrying a different weight.

Here's how it all breaks down, according to the popular FICO scoring model (which most lenders use).

1. Payment History (35%)

This is the most important piece of the puzzle.
Lenders want to know: *Do you pay your bills on time?* Even one late payment can hurt, so

consistency is key. Think of this as your trust factor.

2. Amounts Owed (30%)

Also known as your credit utilization. It looks at how much of your available credit you're actually using. Keeping your balances low (ideally under 10%) shows you're managing things wisely, not living off borrowed money.

3. Length of Credit History (15%)

The longer you've had credit, the better. Lenders like seeing a solid track record over time. That's why it's smart to keep older accounts open, even if you don't use them much anymore.

4. New Credit (10%)

Every time you apply for a new credit card or loan, a hard inquiry shows up on your report. A few here and there is no big deal, but applying for a bunch of accounts at once can make it look like you're in financial trouble.

5. Credit Mix (10%)

Lenders love variety. Having a mix of credit cards, auto loans, student loans, etc., shows that you can handle different kinds of debt responsibly.

It's like saying, *"I've got experience with more than one financial tool."*

6. Recent Activity (Bonus Points!)

Not officially part of the core FICO formula, but still worth noting. Paying off a big debt, resolving a past issue, or clearing up collections can lead to a quick score bump. It's like your report saying, "Hey, they're making moves in the right direction!"

A strong credit report would typically show:

- 100% On-Time Payment History
- Low Credit Usage (Below 10%)
- No Collections, Bankruptcies, or Legal Judgments
- Credit Age of at least 5yrs 9mos Minimal
- Hard Inquiries (preferably fewer than 3 in the past 2 years)
- A Healthy Mix of Credit Types

Why What's Behind Your Score
Matters More Than the Number

A lot of people get caught up chasing that "magic number" —whether it's 700, 750, or 800. But here's the real deal: your score is just the surface. The stuff underneath—your actual habits and history—is what really tells your financial story.

Think about this:

Someone with a 710 score and a brand-new credit profile, but a spotless payment history, might actually look less favorable than someone with a 680 score but has a longer credit history and a more robust credit mix.

Two people might both have a 700, but one could be buried in debt, while the other barely owes a thing. Same number, very different situations.

And don't forget: some lenders go beyond the score. They'll manually review your full report to see how you really handle money, not just where you land on the number line.

So instead of stressing over the score alone, focus on building strong, consistent habits. The number will follow, and you'll have a solid foundation lenders can trust.

Bottom Line:

If you stick to smart credit habits, like paying on time, keeping your balances low, and not overdoing it with new accounts, your score will usually fall right into place. At the end of the day, it's not just about chasing a number. It's your everyday financial behavior that builds real trust, and that's what opens doors to the things you want in life.

Chapter 2
Debt - Slavery vs Freedom

*The Truth About Good Debt, Bad Debt, and
Breaking the Chains*

I still remember the first time I heard someone say, "Debt is a tool." I was totally confused. A tool? Debt is the worst thing ever, next to taxes. At least that's what I was taught. Growing up, it was drilled into me that debt was something to fear. Once you get into it, your life would be ruined forever. In fact, I once heard debt referred to as financial slavery.

Like most parents, my mom taught me that if you don't have the cash, you cannot afford it, and credit cards are bad. Later, I came to learn that my mom had credit cards, and most times had them maxed out because money was tight and she needed to use them just to make ends meet. Not making much money, often, she was only able to make the minimum payments, which, as you can imagine, did nothing in paying down the debt. Because my mom didn't know how to properly use debt, she ended up trapped in this debt cycle, seeing no way out.

I remember here saying she felt like she was working just to pay the bills and was not getting ahead. She told me, "Credit cards are just like trouble, easy to get into and hard to get out. So naturally, I grew up thinking debt is bad and I must stay away from it at all cost.

But here's the thing: that's not the full picture.

We've been told debt is slavery, —and in many ways, that's true. Especially the way most of us use it. But what I've come to realize is that debt can either bind you or free you, depending on how you use it. Actually, debt is more like a key; you can use it to lock you down or to open endless opportunities.

Let me break this down to help you understand what I mean.

What We've Been Told About Debt

We've been told to avoid debt like it's a virus. "Don't borrow unless it's an emergency." "If you can't pay cash, you can't afford it." "Credit cards will ruin your life." Sound familiar?

I get it, most of that advice came from love. Our parents and grandparents lived through times when borrowing meant you were desperate. My grandma even quoted the bible to me regarding debt. Romans 13:8 "Owe no man anything…" but that is where the verse stops for most people. That is where the misinterpretation happens. The rest of the verse says "…but to love one another". Actually, the scripture is not about debt, but the importance of loving one another. My granddad used to say, "Owe a man money, and you're working for him, not yourself." And to a great extent, he wasn't wrong.

But nobody explained the other side of the coin. The part where debt, when used smartly, could actually help you build wealth, start a business, take advantage of financial opportunities, or even retire early.

In the name of love and protection, they gave us warnings, but left out the most important part, the strategy.

It's like someone handing you a chainsaw and only yelling, "Don't cut your leg off" without teaching you how to actually use it to build a shelter or make firewood to keep warm. So, we either fear debt entirely or we misuse it out of ignorance.

Good Debt vs. Bad Debt: Learning the Difference

Okay, so here's the truth: not all debt is created equal. Some debt is like eating your vegetables. We may not like to eat them, but they are necessary to be healthy. Other debt is like eating candy; it feels good in the moment, but if you eat too much, you'll regret it.

Let's take a look at bad debt.

The number one culprit of bad debt is consumer debt. This is when you buy stuff that doesn't grow in value, like clothes, gadgets, or vacations, on high-interest credit cards or loans. If we are being honest, most consumer debt is used to impress others or to make us feel better about ourselves or our circumstances.

For example, if you bought a $1,500 TV on a credit card with 24% interest and was not able to pay it off before the interest kicks in (30 days), that, my friend, is the definition of bad debt. Or perhaps you see something that is on sale, but you don't have the money to pay for it, so you use your credit card, because it's a "good deal. You convince yourself you are saving money. The truth is, you were not saving money; you were misusing debt as a consumer.

Now, good debt is a different story.

Good debt is money you borrow to make more money. It's the kind of debt that fuels growth, not consumption.

Examples of this are student loans (depending on your area of study), real estate mortgages, or a loan to buy or start a business.

Let me give you an example: I bought my first rental property using a mortgage. I only put 20% down. The bank covered the rest. Every month, my tenants pay rent that covers my mortgage payment, and then some. That extra income is profit. And that property is appreciating over time. So technically, I'm in debt, but that debt is working for me, not against me. That's good debt in action.

Of course, student loans can be a grey area. If you're studying something with a high earning potential, like engineering, tech, or medicine, then the debt is often worth it. But if you're borrowing six figures to major in something that doesn't guarantee a decent income…well, let's just say I've got friends still paying off degrees they barely use.

How I Learned to Leverage Debt for Freedom

As I began to study the strategies of the rich and the wealthy (yes, there is a difference), I began to realize they were not afraid to use debt (O.P.M.) to buy cash-flowing assets to increase their financial situations. Some of the wealthiest people you may know of do not use their money to invest. They understand the power of leverage and opportunity cost. Once I realized this is how successful people play the game, I understood the power of debt and how it can be like fire. It can either warm you or burn you. It just depends on whether you have the knowledge on how to use it.

The turning point came when I started treating debt like a business partner. I stopped using credit to cover emotional spending or to impress others and started using it to build wealth. I leveraged my low-interest credit cards to launch my online store. I used mortgage debt to purchase real estate to generate monthly income. And I have even used lines of credit to become a Private Lender, creating income for myself, using someone else's money, better known as debt.

Here's what I learned:

- Know the cost of your debt. Evaluate the deal. Does it make sense, meaning, do you make money?
- Make your debt earn. If you're going to borrow, it should be for something that pays you back-more than it costs.
- Use other people's money strategically. That's what banks do. That's what investors do. And if you play it smart, you can do it too.
- Never borrow for lifestyle upgrades, period. That fancy car or designer bag feels great for a month and weighs on your soul for years. Your assets should pay for these things.

Now, I'm not saying you need to go out and rack up debt to get rich. What I'm saying is: don't fear debt, understand it. Learn the rules of the game and use them to your advantage.

Chapter 3
Scaling with OPM: The Key Strategy Behind Building Wealth

How the Wealthy Get Rich Without Spending Their Own Money

Let's talk about one of the biggest secrets wealthy people swear by but no one teaches us in school: OPM, which stands for "Other People's Money."

Now, before your eyes glaze over or you think this is some slick investment trick for billionaires in suits, hear me out. OPM is something everyday people use all the time, — some of us just don't realize we're doing it. If you've ever used a mortgage to buy a house, guess what? You've used OPM. Welcome to the club.

At its core, using OPM means using someone else's money to build your own wealth. It's like borrowing a shovel to dig your financial well faster. You don't have to own the shovel to benefit from the water, right?

Myths That Keep People Stuck

When I first started hearing about OPM, I had my doubts. I thought, "Isn't that something only big-time investors or companies do? Don't you have to already be rich or have connections?" And let's not forget the classic from the previous chapter: "Debt is bad. Period."

But here's the truth: using OPM <u>wisely</u> isn't about being rich, and it's definitely not about being reckless. It's about understanding the game. This isn't some get-rich-quick nonsense. It's a legit strategy that can change your financial trajectory, if you know how to use it strategically.

Real-Life Forms of OPM

So, how does this play out in real life? OPM comes in many flavors. Sometimes it's credit, like business credit cards or personal loans. Other times, it's money from investors, maybe a family member who believes in your idea, or a partner who brings capital to the table.

There's also bank financing. Think mortgages, lines of credit, or business loans. And don't sleep on government-backed programs. Have you ever heard of SBA loans or grants? Those are all forms of OPM. Even tapping into the equity in your house or your stock portfolio can be a form of OPM.

The point is, you've got more options than you think. The key is knowing which one fits your goal and your risk tolerance.

The Rule You Can't Ignore

Here's the golden rule when it comes to using OPM: it should make you money.

Let's keep it simple. If you borrow money and it costs you more than it brings in, you've got a problem. That's not leveraging. That's just digging a deeper hole.

But if you borrow money to build something, whether that's real estate, a small business, or a side hustle that generates real income, now you're using OPM the smart way.

It's the difference between borrowing $10,000 to flip a house and make a $15,000 profit or borrowing that same $10,000 to go on a two-week luxury vacation. One is an investment. The other is just expensive escapism.

Getting Ready to Use OPM Like a Pro

Before you go borrowing money left and right, let's talk prep. Because lenders and investors don't just hand out money for dreams, they want to see a plan.

First off, clean up your credit. That's the first thing anyone will check. And don't just stop at good credit, —make sure it's structured right. That means low balances, no late payments, and a healthy credit mix.

Then, have a clear, actionable plan. Know exactly what you'll do with the money, how it will make you income, and how you'll pay it back. Be able to explain it in one sentence. "I'm using $5,000 to buy a vending machine route that makes $1,500 a month." Boom. That's a plan.

Also, remember, people invest in people. So, build trust. Whether it's a bank, a buddy, or a business partner, your reliability matters more than your pitch deck.

And whatever you do, know the terms. Interest rates, payback periods, equity splits, etc. Read every line, remember "the big print giveth, the small print taketh away". Ask questions. If you don't understand something, don't fake it. It's your money and reputation on the line.

Start Small

You don't need to make a million-dollar move to get started. In fact, I recommend you don't.

Test the waters with something small but strategic. Got a 0% APR credit card offer? Maybe that's your chance to buy inventory for an online store. This is how I got my first online store. Do you know a friend who wants to co-invest in a business? That is how I got my second online store. That's OPM in action.

You can even take a personal loan to buy a piece of cash-flowing equipment, like a bounce house you rent out on weekends or photography gear for freelance gigs. Use that borrowed money to create more income.

Whatever you do, master one move before you try to scale. The cliché of "multiple streams of income" is misunderstood and misrepresented. Yes, the wealthy do have multiple streams of income, but *after* creating a consistent flow of income by focusing on one thing first. After they have systems in place to have that business run with little to no effort from them, they focus on the next opportunity.

This is something I learned the hard way. I invested in three online stores and started a trucking and logistics company, while still operating my financial services practice. I was chasing passive income, which doesn't exist, at least initially, when starting a business. Learn the ropes, know your numbers, and create systems. Then, and only then, you can begin to diversify to create multiple streams of income.

Scaling Up: The Power of Momentum

Once you have successfully created cash flow with one opportunity, and if you're disciplined, you can reinvest those profits into your next OPM-funded venture.

Say you borrowed $10K, turned it into $20K, and paid off the debt. Now you've got proof of concept and profit. That's what banks and investors love. Do that a few times, and you're no longer just borrowing, you're building. Remember to always know your numbers. If the math ever stops making sense, don't double down out of ego. Know when to pause, pivot, or even walk away. The key to scaling is knowing when not to.

The Other Side of the Coin: The Risks

Let's keep it real, OPM is powerful, but it's not without risk. Borrowing money without a clear, tested plan can backfire hard. You could end up owing more than you can handle, especially if the income stream you hoped for doesn't show up. Now you find yourself struggling to pay back the money and potentially jeopardizing your credit, which is a cornerstone to your financial success.

And then there's the emotional weight. Owing others, whether it's a bank, a friend, or a family member, can be very stressful. Especially if things go sideways.

That's why I always say: have a Plan B on how you will be able to repay the money borrowed. I know you feel you have thought of everything and there is no way this opportunity can fail, however, I have learned, when it comes to business, whatever can go wrong, will go wrong. Plan for success but prepare for reality.

Wealth Is a Team Sport

Here's the real takeaway: collaboration beats competition. Don't feel you have to do it by yourself. Often, many people feel they must create success in a vacuum. Perhaps you feel you have something to prove and don't want to ask for help. Building wealth is a game. The faster you learn the rules and how to play, the faster you can get to your financial freedom. It is often said, "it takes money to make money". This is true, however, it doesn't have to be your money. If you have a great idea, a good strategy, and a vetted business plan, you can find the money. Don't let your ego or lack of money stop you from building wealth.

Summary

So, you're feeling ready to make a move with OPM? That's great, but before you jump in, make sure you've checked a few important boxes. First, your credit should be in good shape, not just free of issues, but structured well enough to attract lenders or investors. Next, be sure your plan is crystal clear. Vague dreams don't get funded, but actionable, income-producing ideas do.

Know exactly how the money you're borrowing is going to work for you and avoid using it for things that lose value or drain your cash. It also helps to double-check the fine print: interest rates, repayment terms, and hidden fees. Those details matter. Borrowing someone else's money is a responsibility, but when you're prepared, it's a tool that can open doors most people never walk through. Make sure you're not just chasing a shortcut but stepping into a strategy.

Chapter 4
The Harsh Truth: You Might Be Giving Your Money Away

Ever look at your bank account and think:
"Wait... where did it all go?"

I remember a time when I'd check my bank account and feel like someone was stealing my money. I know I'd just got paid, but my account looked as if the check had not been deposited. You know what I'm talking about? Your paycheck hit on Friday. You pay your rent and a few other bills you planned to pay with this check. Go out with friends to catch up and unwind on Saturday. Run to the grocery store to purchase groceries and a few necessities on Sunday. Monday, you go to the ATM to get some cash, and you see your balance and wonder, "Didn't I just get paid on Friday"?

It didn't make sense. I wasn't out here buying yachts. I wasn't being reckless. But something was off. That's when I realized: I wasn't broke because I didn't make enough money. I was broke because I didn't know where it was going.

And maybe you've been there too, wondering how someone with a decent income still feels like they're drowning. The truth? You're probably not broke. You're just leaking.

When I Finally Understood Cash Flow

It all started clicking when I learned about cash flow. Not in the corporate "quarterly earnings" kind of way, but in the "I have to wait until I get paid" kind of way.

Cash flow is simple. It's what comes in, minus what goes out. That's it. That little (or big) number left over after the bills and the spending? That's your breathing room. That's what decides if you're calm or constantly scrambling.

At one point, my own "flow" was more like a drip. I had money coming in, after all, my business was making money. But it was flowing out just as fast. I had no idea where it was going. So, I started tracking every dollar. Every swipe. Every auto-payment. At first, I started with an Excel spreadsheet. As you can imagine, it was tedious and time-consuming. However, I was determined to see where my money was going. Eventually, I came across an app that did all of it for me, which made it easier and required a fraction of the time to see where my money was going. Guess what I discovered? I was leaking money like the Titanic.

The Money Leaks That Nearly Sank Me

First, let's talk about subscriptions. Have you ever wanted to watch a movie on a streaming platform, but you didn't have a subscription? No worries, we just sign up for the 7-day free trial. You know the rest of the story. How about the workout apps that promise to get you toned and lean in 30days or the weight loss app that tells you what to eat, when to eat it, and how much to eat. You must get this app because you are really going to stick to it this time. The other 3 apps were "not for you". Finally, the apps you don't even remember subscribing to at all. Because the individual amounts are so small, we don't even see them when they come out of our bank account or post to our credit cards.

Next is dining out. We tend not to think about the casual $12 - $15 lunches or quick carry-out on the way home. We like to focus on the major splurge when we go to the really nice restaurants and spend over $50 on a meal, all in the name of "you only live once" or "I work hard,

I deserve to treat myself". These convenience meals or well-deserved dinners can add up fast.

But the biggest leak of all?   Interest payments on credit cards. I didn't realize the amount of money I was paying in interest by just making the minimum payment each month on my credit cards. Often, we deceive ourselves into thinking that if we can afford the minimum payment, we can afford to buy the item.

For example, the minimum payment on a $500 purchase using a credit card with a 24% interest rate is only $15/month. Seems pretty affordable. However, it will take you 10 years to pay off the $500 and cost you $1300 in interest. When I saw how much money I was paying monthly in interest, I could not believe it. I was literally giving my money away to the credit card companies. That's when it hit me: I didn't have a plan for my money, so it was making one for itself.

The Shift: Giving Every Dollar a Job

I knew I had to begin to do things differently. Not by living like a hermit or not enjoying life, but by being intentional. I enjoy nice things and love to travel. I never really bought into the mindset of the millionaire next door, where I only bought or did things based solely on necessity. Nor having to deny my family or myself some of the "wants" we desired. I realized with discipline and structure, I could create the lifestyle I desired.

So, I tried something called zero-based budgeting. Don't let the name scare you, it just means every dollar you earn has a role. Whether it's for rent, savings, groceries, or fun, it all gets accounted for. No money just sitting around being lazy. I broke things down into three categories:

1. Essentials (bills, food, gas)
2. Future (savings, debt payments, investments)
3. Flex (fun, travel, impulse stuff, but planned impulse, if that makes sense)

And then I automated the boring stuff. Savings went out the minute I got paid. Bills were put on autopay, and investing was also on autopilot. I even set little alerts on my bank app to ping me when I spent too much in certain areas. It was like building a fence around my financial chaos. And it worked.

A Simple Ritual That Changed Everything

Once a week, on Sunday, I check the reports on my app to see actual spending from last week, look ahead to what's coming up, and make a few adjustments when necessary. It is amazing how this one change helps me to manage my finances with no guilt, no stress, and peace of mind. I'm sure it also has saved me hundreds, probably thousands, and more importantly, it gave me back control.

The Freedom of Flowing Right

Once I plugged those leaks, something magical happened. I stopped feeling anxious about money. I stopped needing to "treat myself" to feel better. Because having financial peace was a treat. And when you get into positive cash flow territory, even just a little bit, everything shifts. You start dreaming bigger. You start saving, not out of fear, but out of excitement. You start seeing money as a tool.

If you're tired of that Monday morning mystery, that "where the heck did it all go" feeling, then maybe it's time to flip the script. Your money doesn't need more hustle. It needs more intention. You already work hard. It's time your money did too. So start small. Track every dollar for 30 days. No shame, no pressure, just curiosity. Because once you see where it's going, you'll start deciding where it should go. And that's the moment you stop surviving and start thriving.

Chapter 5
Alternative Investments —
Putting Your Money to Work

Your dollars shouldn't just sit; they should sweat.

Why Your Money Deserves a Side Hustle

There was a time when I felt pretty proud of myself for finally building a savings cushion. I was doing the "responsible" thing, parking money in a high-yield savings account. I checked it after six months, expecting to see some decent growth. What I quickly realized was, although I was getting a higher interest rate on my money than traditional savings accounts, it was not going to change my financial situation. That's when it hit me: saving is smart, for short-term goals, but letting your money sit in a bank, earning single-digit interest, is not the way to achieve financial freedom. I needed to find opportunities where I could earn double-digit returns.

Most of us work hard for every dollar, but very few of us require our dollars to work for us. Many of us were taught to take pride in working hard to make money. However, the truth is to learn how to have your money work harder than you. When people with a poor mindset need more money, the first thing they think about is what they can do to earn more money: work overtime, pick up another job, etc. However, when individuals with a wealthy mindset need more money, they think about more ways to have their money earn more money. The goal should be to put your money to work, so you don't have to. I have a saying, "Every day you are either earning money or losing money". The value of the dollar is consistently decreasing due to inflation. If it is not earning more than inflation, you are losing money. Also, don't forget about the taxes you must pay on the interest earned in that account. Therefore, you cannot afford to let it sit in a savings account earning 1%-3%. You are losing money, but you think you are doing a good thing. In fact, you are slowly sliding into financial ruin.

We're often taught that traditional investments like stocks and bonds are the main way to grow wealth. But that's only part of the picture. There's a whole world of investments outside that bubble. They're called alternative investments, and they're not just for the rich. They're for people who want to diversify, grow their money faster, and maybe even earn while they sleep (creating passive income).

What Are Alternative Investments

Let's keep it simple. An alternative investment is just about anything that isn't a stock, bond, or savings account. If you've ever bought a rental property, dabbled in crypto, or even collected something you believe will go up in value, congrats, you've touched the world of alternative investments. Unlike traditional investments, which often follow the stock market's rollercoaster, alternatives don't always move in sync with the markets. That's part of their appeal. From rental properties and REITs to lending platforms, business equity, digital currencies, precious metals, and even farmland, these are the tools that can help your money grow in ways traditional advice never taught you.

It's not about being fancy or trendy. It's about seeing opportunities where others aren't looking and understanding that accumulating wealth has more than one path.

Why Consider Alternatives?

For one, alternative investments can help protect you when the market takes a dive. Stocks may tank, but your rental income doesn't disappear just because Wall Street had a bad week. Alternatives don't all move together, and that lower correlation can create stability when the economy feels uncertain.

Then there's the income factor. Some alternatives can pay you while you wait for them to appreciate. For example, let's look at a rental property. Your tenant's rent checks provide you with a monthly income, while the overall value of the property is going up over time. How about loan interest or dividends from a private lending investment. That's cash in your pocket, not just theoretical gains on a screen.

And let's not forget the personal element. You can align your money with what you care about. If you're passionate about real estate, you can invest in it. If you love wine or art, or sustainability, there are funds and platforms that allow you to put your money where your passion lies. It's not just about growing wealth; it's about doing it in a way that feels connected to your life and your purpose.

Real Estate: Bricks, Mortar, and Monthly Rent

I remember when I bought a beat-up single-family home on the south side of Chicago. Many people told me it was not a good investment. The place needed work, the backyard was a jungle, and it had been empty for some time. I bought it from another investor who planned to do the rehab himself but ran out of money. I was able to help him and get myself a great deal in the process. I purchased it for $20,000 cash. I invested about $30,000 to fix it up (I used OPM). Then I rented it out and refinanced the property, pulling out $65,000 in order to pay off the short-term loan, pay myself back my initial investment of $20,000, and still had approximately $10,000 in my pocket after paying closing costs. Now I own a cash-flowing asset, free and clear, that generates me income every month and increases in value.

That's the magic of real estate. Whether you're buying to rent, flipping for profit, or investing in REITs, it's one of the most accessible and familiar forms of alternative investing. It can generate income, build equity, and give you leverage to scale over time. And the tax benefits are amazing.

But let's be real, it's not all rainbows and sunshine. Tenants call at midnight. Repairs pop up when you least expect them. And if the market turns or a property sits vacant, the bills don't stop. That's why it's important to run the numbers, start small, and understand your comfort level before diving in.

Private Lending and Peer-to-Peer Platforms

Imagine turning the tables and being the one who earns interest instead of paying it. That's what private lending and peer-to-peer investing are all about. You provide the capital, someone else borrows it, and you get paid back, with interest.

It's not foolproof. Some borrowers default, and your return depends heavily on the platform or the terms of the deal. This is why I focus on collateralized opportunities only. That means, if the borrower defaults, I have a lien on the real estate or equity in the business. When done correctly, this type of investing can create a steady monthly income. It's like being the bank. This option works well for those who are analytical, cautious, and don't mind reviewing deals. But if the idea of someone not paying you back makes you panic, this might not be the best fit for your first step into alternatives.

Investing in Businesses Without Running One

You don't have to launch a startup to get a piece of one. Through angel investing or private equity funds, you can back early-stage companies and potentially ride the wave if they grow. The risk here is real. Most startups don't make it. But if one does, the payoff can be enormous, think Uber, Facebook, Amazon, etc. The key is to invest in what you understand and only use money you can afford to lose. This is high-risk, high-reward territory, and it's not about instant returns, it's about believing in the long game. If you've got a nose for innovation and a desire to support ideas you believe in, this can be a powerful way to grow wealth while helping others build theirs.

The Wild World of Crypto and Digital Assets

Crypto isn't just a buzzword anymore. It's a new financial frontier, and whether you love it or hate it, it's here to stay. At its core, crypto is digital money, —decentralized, borderless, and incredibly volatile. Bitcoin and Ethereum are the big names, but thousands of digital assets exist, each with its own use case and community. Some people jump in chasing big gains. I chose to invest in crypto because I understood the technology and the future of our monetary system. Again, I was told by friends and family I was crazy, and I was throwing away my money. Fast forward several years, and I am so happy I followed my research, and many of them are wishing they had gotten in when I did. Either way, crypto is not something you dive into blindly. It's fast-moving, full of hype, and often misunderstood. If you're curious, start small, educate yourself, and never invest money you can't stomach losing. It's not boring, but it sure is a wild ride.

Things You Can Touch: Art, Gold, and More

There's something satisfying about investing in something you can actually hold. Unlike crypto, tangible assets like gold, silver, rare art, and even vintage watches offer a different kind of value, one that doesn't rely on algorithms or the stock markets. These kinds of investments can act as hedges against inflation and economic uncertainty. They're not always easy to liquidate, and you need to understand what makes them valuable. But for some people, especially collectors, this can be a perfect blend of passion and portfolio. They are also used by those who know how to minimize or eliminate taxes and pass along wealth. I have put my toe in this arena as well with the purchase of art and watches. Not sure how I will fare with the watches because I have learned a lot more since I made my first few purchases, but I am confident I did well with the art purchases. Just be cautious. Sentimental value doesn't always translate to market value. Know what you're buying, and think with both your heart and your head.

Risks, Scams, and Common-Sense Safeguards

Let's not sugarcoat it, alternative investments carry risk. And because they're less regulated, they can attract shady characters and overhyped deals. If you don't fully understand how the investment works, don't put your money in it. And if everyone else is jumping on the same trend without asking questions, slow down and do your research. It may be as good as they say, or you may be following the sheep to slaughter. Your best protection is to verify, not FOMO (Fear of Missing Out). Due diligence isn't optional. It's the line between building wealth and getting burned. Ask questions, read everything, and never feel rushed into a deal. Your money, your rules.

Build an Alternative Investment Plan That Fits Your Life

This isn't about jumping into ten different things at once. It's about finding what works for you and starting small. If you're cautious, maybe a REIT or a small real estate platform investment is your first step. If you're bold and curious, you might explore crypto or private lending. The key is to know yourself, your risk tolerance, your financial goals, and how involved you want to be. There are investments out here for everyone, you just have to find what's best for you.

But, by all means, whatever you do, give every dollar a job. Your money should earn money for you, so someday you no longer have to work a job to pay for your lifestyle. Your investments will generate the money to cover your expenses. Once you achieve this, you now have financial freedom.

Don't Just Save — Activate Your Dollars

Saving is safe. But wealth? That's built by motion. By putting your money in places where it can stretch, grow, and work even when you're not. Alternative investments might seem intimidating at first, but once you understand the landscape, they become exciting. They give you options, cash flow, and creative control. They remind you that you don't have to follow the same path everyone else is walking.

So, here's your challenge. Pick one alternative investment you've never explored and commit to spending some time learning about it. No pressure to act. Just start the conversation. Because the moment you stop treating your money like it needs protection and start treating it like a partner, that's when everything changes.

Chapter 6
Tax Efficiency: It's Not How Much You Make

It's how much you keep

The High Earner Who Still Struggled

A few years ago, I had a client who, on paper, had it all. Let's call him Jason. He was earning just north of $350,000 a year, working as a senior C-Suite Executive at a big-name marketing agency here in Chicago. He had the title, the salary, the benefits, the prestige. Everyone assumed he was doing great.

But Jason had a secret. He was stressed. Not because of the work, —he loved his job. He was stressed because his bank account never seemed to reflect the life people thought he had. Every month, he felt like he was playing catch-up. Between the mortgage, car note, loan payments, taxes, and the occasional splurge just to keep up appearances, his savings were minimal, and investing felt out of reach. I remember one time he said to me: "I'm making more than I ever dreamed of, but it's like the money disappears before I even touch it." Now you may say, perhaps he was living beyond his means or trying to keep up with the Joneses. After reviewing Jason's complete financial situation, I came to realize Jason didn't have a spending problem. He had a tax problem. Now, sure, he could have benefited from spending less money in certain areas, but why do we work so hard in the first place? To enjoy some of the finer things in life, have great experiences, and create wonderful memories. At least that's how I feel about it. When working with my clients, we work to design a plan around the lifestyle and experiences they desire, not to have a certain amount of money sitting in the bank. It is my belief that money is just a tool to facilitate the creation of the life you desire. It is not to be hoarded or squandered. Anyway, Jason's issue was that he was working hard, but his money wasn't. He had a massive leak in his financial boat. The government was getting a large cut of his money before he even saw it in the form of taxes. We're taught that in order to live the life we desire, we must chase income, climb the corporate ladder, and find more ways to "work" for money. But the truth is, income doesn't equal wealth. Not if too much of it slips through your fingers on the way to your bank account. The key is to learn how to stop giving away your money (see chapter 4).

Understanding the Tax Game

Let's get one thing clear, taxes are the biggest adversary of wealth. The tax code can be very complex and confusing. It is also known to frustrate most people who don't take the time to understand how it works. There are different types of taxes; federal, state, and even local, and they all want a piece. Your paycheck is just the starting point. The government takes a chunk based on how much you earn, but also how your income is structured. This is where things get interesting. The IRS doesn't care how many hours you worked or how valuable your contribution is to society. They only care about the type of income you have and how it's reported. There are three categories: earned income, passive income, and portfolio income.

A great example of earned income is your paycheck. You work, you get paid, and Uncle Sam takes his taxes out first, before you get to spend a dime. This is the worst form of income because you have very few ways to minimize the amount of taxes you pay. It's the most straightforward and the least tax-efficient. It would be great if the taxes stopped there, but it doesn't. We continue to pay taxes on money we have already paid taxes on. Think about it, when you go to the grocery store, purchase gas, buy clothes, purchase a home or automobile, you pay more taxes. It is no wonder that the working class finds it so hard to get ahead. Most of their income is taken by taxes.

This isn't to cause a feeling of hopelessness for you if you are in this category. However, it is to make you aware of why it seems like the more you make, it still doesn't seem to be enough. As quickly as you can, you must learn a way to reduce the amount of income you make in this income type.

An example of Passive income is rental income or royalties from creative works, where you do not materially participate. Passive income is generally taxed at the same rate as your Earned Income; however, it often comes with fewer tax strings and can sometimes be offset by expenses or depreciation. Then there's portfolio income, which includes things like stocks, bonds, and other securities.

Examples of Portfolio Income (Investment Income) are dividends, interest payments, and capital gains. Capital gains are taxed differently depending on how long you hold the asset. If you hold an asset, say a stock, art, or a piece of real estate, for over a year, then sell it, the gain from selling it is taxed at a lower rate called Long-Term Capital Gains. At the time of writing this book, the average capital gains tax is 15%. This simple distinction, how long you hold something, can make a huge difference. If you were to sell the asset in one year or less, your profits would be taxed as "ordinary income" and taxed at your marginal tax bracket, which you pay on your earned income. Knowing this simple strategy can save you thousands in taxes.

What matters isn't just the amount you earn. It's the source of income. Each source is taxed differently, which can cause more loss of income. There's also the hidden cost, which is opportunity cost. Money you could've had working for you, but instead, it slipped away because you didn't know any better.

Why Tax Efficiency Matters

Think about two people earning the same amount. Let's say $100,000 each. One has a traditional job, pays full income taxes, and ends up taking home around $70,000 after everything is said and done. The other earns part of their income through investments, contribute strategically to retirement accounts, and takes advantage of deductions available to small business owners. They walk away with closer to $85,000 in usable cash. Same earnings, different outcomes. All because one of them took the time to learn how structure their income to minimize their taxes, by understanding the tax code.

When your tax-efficient, you're not just saving money, you're speeding up your path to wealth. That extra $10,000 or $15,000 every year is money you can invest, save, or put toward building something meaningful. Over time, it compounds into real financial freedom. Neglecting tax planning comes with a huge cost. There's the obvious stuff like owing more in April than you expected, or missing out on deductions that could've lowered your taxable income.

The Power of Business Ownership

When people talk about the tax advantages of owning a business, it can sound like a loophole. But it's not, it's intentional and strategic. The tax code is designed to reward people who take risks, create jobs, and invest in building things. Starting a side hustle, even something small, opens a new world of deductions and financial flexibility. Maybe you sell digital products online. Maybe you tutor or freelance. Whatever the case, the moment it becomes a business, certain expenses that were once personal can become professional expenses. Think about your cell phone, your internet, the software you use, and even part of your rent or mortgage if you work from home. These are all potentially deductible when tied to your business. You're not doing anything shady. You're just shifting the way your expenses are categorized, in a way that the law allows and encourages. This is why I strongly encourage everyone to start a business. In addition, if there are any business losses or start-up costs, you can reduce the amount of taxes you pay on your W-2 income.

But the biggest benefit of having a business, unlike W-2 income, you get to write off as many business expenses as you can, then you are taxed on what is left. So, if you work with a tax strategist to plan your taxes throughout the year, you can be like the wealthy and not pay any income tax (at least minimize the amount you pay).

It's not about cheating the system. It's about understanding the tax code and playing the game with intention. By shifting more of your income to come from sources that are taxed less aggressively, you gain control over your financial trajectory.

Timing is Everything

Tax planning isn't just about what you do. It's about when you do it. The timing of your income and expenses can dramatically affect your bottom line. If you sell investments at a loss, you can use those losses to offset gains elsewhere. That's called tax-loss harvesting. If you expect to be in a lower tax bracket next year, you might defer a bonus or income until then. If you have business expenses coming up, paying them before year-end could reduce this year's taxable income. These may sound like minor moves, but they add up. With taxes, small shifts can mean big differences.

Common Mistakes to Avoid

Too many people leave money on the table without realizing it. One way is to contribute to retirement accounts. Now, I am not in favor of "over-funding" your employer-sponsored retirement accounts. Just max out the amount your employer will match. Also, contribute to the Health Savings Account (HSA), if one is offered. Also, some people file under the wrong tax status, not realizing that being the head of household or qualifying for certain credits could save them thousands. Another missed opportunity is sticking with the same tax withholdings all year, even after a raise, a move, or a major life change, and end up with a surprise tax bill. The tax system doesn't adjust itself for you. You must keep tabs on your life and make sure your tax setup keeps pace. It's not hard, but it does require awareness or working with someone who understands the tax system.

Get Help, — You Don't Have to Go It Alone

If this all sounds overwhelming, that's okay. You're not expected to become a tax expert. But you are expected to care. Hiring a tax professional, preferably a tax strategist, can transform your entire tax situation. Unlike a tax preparer, who just reports to the IRS what has already happened, a tax strategist helps you see the opportunities you didn't know existed. And the money you spend on their services is often a fraction of what you'll save by using a smarter strategy.

Final Word: Make It a Year-Round Mindset

Here's the truth most people miss, tax planning isn't an event. It's a lifestyle. It's not something you scramble to do in March before the April deadline. It's a year-round process that, when done well, becomes part of how you think about money.

When you're intentional with your taxes, you take back control. You stop leaving your finances up to chance and you start using the system the way it was meant to be used, as a tool to build wealth.

So, here's your challenge. Spend thirty minutes reviewing your income. Ask yourself not just how much you earn, but how you earn it. Look at your income sources. Look at your structure. Try to find the leaks where taxes are causing you to miss out on wealth building. You don't need to overhaul your world today. You just need to start noticing where the opportunities are that will allow you to keep more of your money. Because the moment you stop treating taxes as a once-a-year headache and start treating them like a strategy, that's when the real wealth-building begins.

Chapter 7
Wealth Preservation: You've Made It, Now How Do You Protect It?

It's not just about building wealth; it's about making sure it stays yours.

The Silent Goal of Wealth

When most people talk about money, the focus is always on how to earn more, invest more, and grow more. But there comes a point when the goal shifts from accumulation to preservation. After years of pushing, saving, and investing, I found myself asking a different question: How do I make sure I don't lose what I have gained? Not out of fear, but out of responsibility to myself, my family, and future generations. Preservation matters just as much as accumulation. Because once you've reached a certain level of financial success, the game changes. It becomes less about offense, chasing the next opportunity, and more about defense, making sure what you've earned isn't eroded, taken, or lost. This requires a different set of skills than you used to acquire your wealth. Let's explore.

The Mindset Shift: Defense Over Offense

When you are focused on the accumulation phase, it's all about growing your net worth through income, investments, and strategic financial decisions. This requires you to be a bit assertive, a risk-taker, very optimistic, and resilient. Once you enter the preservation phase, you must begin to think differently. Now it's all about defense; asset protection, minimizing taxes, liquidity, insurance, and succession planning. If you fail to make this mental shift, you can find yourself back where you started or worse, leaving your heirs exposed to blind spots. In this chapter, I will merely touch the surface of the key areas you must address when you enter the wealth preservation phase. My goal is to provide you with some direction and insight, not conclusive remedies in each area.

The Enemies of Wealth Preservation

There's a misconception that once you make it, the hard part is over. The truth is, maintaining wealth comes with its own set of challenges. If you don't know what you're up against and how to plan for these things, you can lose ground fast.

Asset Protection Basics

So, what does it mean to protect your assets? It's not just about locking money away. It's about structuring your life legally and financially in a way that limits exposure and maximizes control. This is achieved by using various legal structures. If your personal and business assets are all mixed together, you're asking for trouble. Legal structures like LLCs, Trusts, and Charitable Foundations create boundaries between you and your assets, between risk and safety. Each of these vehicles not only helps fortify your assets from lawsuits, judgments, and creditors, but they also provide various degrees of tax efficiency. Word of caution; all trusts are not the same and therefore do not provide the same benefits. A revocable trust allows you to maintain control of the assets and functions as your alter ego. The primary use of a revocable trust is to avoid probate. An irrevocable trust helps you to avoid probate, has many tax-minimizing applications, protections from lawsuits and creditors, and can even ensure your heirs don't squander everything you have built.

An acronym I teach to all my clients is O.N.C.E. (Own Nothing, Control Everything).

Tax Planning

Now that you have more assets, tax planning becomes even more important. You must develop a strategy as to how you will handle Estate taxes, Inheritance tax, capital gains, and Required Minimum Distributions. They all play a role in the efficiency of your tax strategy. As I stated in chapter 6, you want to work with a Tax Strategist or Tax Planner, not just a CPA. Tax strategists help you develop tax-reducing plans throughout the year, so when tax season approaches, you know you have maximized your tax position.

Estate Planning:

Your legacy is more than assets; it's intention. Estate planning is how you ensure the people, causes, and values you care about are honored. Without a plan, decisions will be made for you. With one, you stay in control. Without an estate plan, the state will decide how your assets are divided. That process is called **Probate** and can be time-consuming, expensive, and emotionally draining for your loved ones. Having an estate plan allows you to avoid probate and helps ensure your wishes are followed, your family is protected, and legal and financial complications are minimized. When composing your estate plan, you should make sure you have the following documents: Durable Power of Attorney, Healthcare Power of Attorney, Advanced Healthcare Directive, Letter of Intent (End-of-Life Plan), Pour-Over Will, and a Trust.

Insurance

Unfortunately, when people think about insurance, they mainly think it is just for emergencies or when they die. But it's also one of the most effective and affordable tools for wealth protection. Umbrella policies cover liabilities that go beyond your standard home or auto coverage.

Long-term care insurance protects your finances from the high costs of care if you cannot take care of yourself in your latter years. Liability insurance protects your assets if you are found responsible for causing harm or damage to someone or their property. Permanent life insurance, in addition to proving a death benefit to your family for the rest of your life, can also be used when implementing a financial system known as Infinite Banking.

This system is used to provide guaranteed returns on your money. It also allows you to use the money while it is growing, and protect it from any creditors, lawsuits, judgments, or liens. Infinite Banking is a very powerful financial tool that I feel everyone should have as part of their financial plan.

Liquidity

In wealth preservation, liquidity is a must. Whether it is to take advantage of unexpected opportunities or to address emergencies, you must have access to cash without selling off core assets. Tools like HELOCs (Home Equity Lines of Credit), cash-value life insurance, and High Yield Savings Accounts can provide the leverage and flexibility you need.

Succession Planning

Creating wealth is not easy and keeping it in the family is even more challenging. Statistics show that most wealth is lost by the second or third generation. One of the greatest reasons for this is failing to create a succession plan. This is just as important, if not more important, as building your wealth initially. If you are running a business and it is your intention to pass it on to the next generation, you must be intentional about taking the following steps to ensure the transition goes as planned.

Here's what a well-structured succession plan should cover:

Clear Identification of a Successor

Decide who will take over and make sure they are willing and capable of doing so. You may have an idea of who you may want to take over the business, but they have no interest. If they are not interested or available, you must have a backup option.

Timeline and Transition Plan

Set a realistic timeline for when the transition will take place gradually or immediately, and set milestones when various steps will happen: start shadowing you, take over operations, and finally assume full ownership or autonomy. Be sure you are in constant contact with your employees, clients, and vendors to maintain their confidence during the transition.

Business Valuation

Get a formal valuation of the business to know its value. This also helps with the purchase of buy-sell agreements, tax planning, and division of assets, if necessary.

Tax and Estate Planning Coordination

Be certain to speak with your tax strategist and attorney about the impact this transition will have on your estate. You may have to consider gift taxes, capital gains, and estate tax exposure. If the business is owned by the Irrevocable Family Trust, these concerns are avoidable.

Continuity Plan

You will need to create a plan to address how the business will operate if something unexpected happens before a formal transition (e.g., death or incapacitation). This plan should include emergency leadership delegation, access to bank accounts, passwords, client communications, etc.

**Essential Documents in a Business Succession
Plan**

Here are the documents that typically support a
solid succession plan:

☑ **Buy-Sell Agreement**

☑ **Operating Agreement or Shareholder
Agreement**

☑ **Business Valuation Report**

☑ **Successor Training Plan or
Memorandum**

☑ **Owner's Estate Plan**

☑ **Key Person Insurance Policies**

☑ **Letters of Intent (Optional)**

☑ **Emergency Business Continuity
Instructions**

This should not be considered an exhaustive
list, but some of the basics to get you started.
Everyone's situation is different and needs to be
considered when developing your succession
plan. Please consult your team of advisors

collectively to ensure all bases have been covered and potential challenges have been addressed.

Leaving A Legacy Is Not About Money

Inheritance without education is a setup for failure. If your heirs don't know how to manage money, invest wisely, or handle responsibility, wealth can become a burden instead of a blessing. Start teaching them early by talking about family values, generosity, responsibility, and stewardship. These are the traits that are more likely to preserve wealth across generations. Prepare them to handle the opportunity, not just receive it. Consider leaving a legacy video as a powerful complement to your trust document. The video is not binding, but it can be very meaningful. It lets you share your hopes, your history, your lessons, and your story. Remember, wealth preservation isn't passive. It requires you to be intentional and strategic. This is what separates temporary success from a lasting legacy.

Wealth Isn't Just What You Own

Here's the truth: wealth isn't just about accumulating money or assets. In the end, true wealth is about what you pass on. Your values, your wisdom, your impact.

So, as you move forward, remember this: the goal isn't just to grow your wealth. It's to protect it. Not just for you, but for everyone who comes after. Let that be the legacy you build.

Conclusion

Money Moves was written for you, the person who wants to create a better financial situation for themselves and their family. The one who has worked hard, carried responsibilities, and often put others first. My goal was not to overwhelm you with technical jargon but to hand you a roadmap, a starting point you can follow toward financial freedom and legacy.

The truth is, what I've covered here is only the beginning. Credit, debt, investing, taxes, and wealth preservation, each of these topics could fill entire books on their own. What you've read is just a surface-level introduction, designed to spark your awareness and build your confidence.

You don't need to master every detail on your own. In fact, the best journeys are made with a guide. That's why I encourage you to sit down with a trusted financial professional, someone who can walk with you, explain the complexities, and help you apply these strategies to your unique life.

Financial freedom isn't just for the wealthy, it's for anyone willing to take consistent, intentional steps forward. You've already taken one of the biggest steps by finishing this book. That step alone separates you from the majority of people who never take control of their financial future. The rest of your journey will be about applying what you've learned and going deeper in the areas that matter most to your family.

Remember, your legacy is more than the dollars you leave behind. It's the security, wisdom, and opportunity you create for the next generation. You've started the journey, now keep moving forward, one choice at a time.